GOSCINNY AND UDERZO
PRESENT
AN ASTERIX ADVENT[URE]

ASTERIX AND OBELIX ALL AT SEA

WRITTEN AND ILLUSTRATED BY UDERZO
TRANSLATED BY ANTHEA BELL AND DEREK HOCKRIDGE

HODDER AN[D STOUGHTON]

LONDON   SYDNEY   AUCKLAND

To my grandson, Thomas,
and in homage to that great actor,
Kirk Douglas

＊ The power to make people laugh: from an epigram by Caesar on Terence, the Latin poet.

GAULISH VILLAGE

COMPENDIUM

LAUDANUM

AQUARIUM

TOTORUM

ARMORICA

BELGICA

LUTETIA

SPQR

GAUL
(ROMAN CONQUEST)
50 B.C.

CELTICA

PROVINCIA

AQUITANIA

The year is 50 BC. Gaul is entirely occupied by the Romans.
Well, not entirely… One small village of indomitable Gauls still
holds out against the invaders. And life is not easy for the
Roman legionaries who garrison the fortified camps of
Totorum, Aquarium, Laudanum and Compendium…

5

WELL, YOU SEE, CAESAR, THE GALLEY SLAVES ARE REVOLTING...

AND SO ARE YOU! STOP BEEFING!

THEY'RE ONLY A HANDFUL OF MUTINEERS, O CAESAR. THEY'LL NEVER PASS THE FRETUM GADITANUM*

* STRAITS OF GIBRALTAR.

I HOPE NOT, CRUSTACIUS, OR YOU'LL BE IN DIRE STRAITS YOURSELF! GET MOVING, AND PUT SOME BEEF INTO IT!

I'LL SORT EVERYTHING OUT O WONDER OF WONDERS, DIVINE CAESAR!

BIT OF A STICKY INTERVIEW, EH, ADMIRAL?

SLAM!

VICE-ADMIRAL NAUTILUS, YOU'RE A MORON AND A HALF-WIT AND A GREAT GORMLESS GOOF AND YOU'D BETTER GET THAT GALLEY BACK OR YOU'LL BE IN DIRE STRAITS YOURSELF!

IF WORD GETS OUT THAT A BUNCH OF SLAVES STOLE MY OWN GALLEY, I'LL BE THE LAUGHING STOCK OF THE ENTIRE ANCIENT WORLD!

BUT YOU ALREADY ARE, O WONDER OF WONDERS, DIVINE CAESAR!

WHAT DO YOU MEAN, I ALREADY AM?

WELL, REMEMBER THOSE INDOMITABLE GAULS STILL HOLDING OUT AGAINST...?

LOOK YOU CAN LEAVE THE PAST HISTORY OF THE GALLIC WARS TO ME!

8

LATER, SOME WAY OFF IN GAUL...

I HAD A TERRIBLE NIGHTMARE LAST NIGHT, ASTERIX!

YOU DID?

SCRUNCH!

SCRUNCH!

I DREAMED THAT JULIUS CAESAR DECIDED TO WITHDRAW ALL THE GARRISONS SURROUNDING THE VILLAGE!

JUST A TOUCH OF INDIGESTION, OBELIX! I KEEP TELLING YOU NOT TO EAT MORE THAN THREE BOARS BEFORE GOING TO BED!

BUT I CAN'T GET TO SLEEP WITHOUT AT LEAST FOUR INSIDE ME!

WELL IT WAS ONLY A NIGHTMARE! AND EVEN IF YOUR DREAM CAME TRUE...

SCRUNCH!

WHAT DO YOU MEAN, CAME TRUE?!

WHY NOT? WE MIGHT FINALLY GET PEACE WITH HONOUR!

5A

COME ALONG, DOGMATIX! WE WANT NOTHING TO DO WITH THESE POLICIES OF APPEASEMENT!

?!

OH, OBELIX, DON'T BE SO SILLY! I WAS ONLY JOKING!

OH NO, YOU WEREN'T, MISTER ASTERIX!

YOU WERE INSULTING THE MEMORY OF VERCINGETORIX!

HAVE YOU GONE COMPLETELY BONKERS?

RAISE THE ALARM!! THE ROMANS ARE ABOUT TO ATTACK!!

!!!

A GOOD THING THE ROMANS HAVE GOT MORE SENSE THAN YOU, MISTER ASTERIX!

THAT'S FUNNY! THERE WAS NOTHING TO SUGGEST THEY WERE GOING TO ATTACK!

SCRUNCH! SCRUNCH!

5B

I SAW THEM! THE GARRISONS OF ALL FOUR FORTIFIED CAMPS ARE DRAWN UP ON THE OTHER SIDE OF THE FOREST!

!!?

HMMM..

RIGHT! WE MUST BE PREPARED! CAN YOU DOLE OUT THE MAGIC POTION, GETAFIX?

I MADE TWO CAULDRONS JUST IN CASE, ALTHOUGH ONE IS PLENTY!

HURRY UP! NEXT!

THE EFFECTS OF THE POTION NEVER CEASE TO AMAZE ME!

SOMETHING WRONG, OBELIX?

POOR OLD OBELIX! I EXPECT GETAFIX WOULDN'T GIVE HIM ANY MAGIC POTION, AS USUAL!

WE KNOW IT HAD A PERMANENT EFFECT ON HIM... BUT WHAT WOULD HAPPEN IF HE DRANK SOME MORE NOW?

THERE'D BE DANGEROUS SIDE EFFECTS, ASTERIX, AND ALL MY SKILL WOULD BE POWERLESS TO COUNTERACT THEM!

(SOON AFTERWARDS...)

THIS IS ODD, O DRUID! OBELIX IS MISSING!

YOU KNOW HOW TOUCHY HE IS! HE MUST HAVE GONE OFF IN A SULK, BUT I'M SURE HE'LL BE THE FIRST TO GO FOR THE ROMANS.

AS IT HAPPENS, THE ROMANS ARE NOT FAR AWAY. THE FOUR GARRISONS ARE DRAWN UP ON PARADE, BEING REVIEWED BY THEIR NEW COMMANDER, VICE-ADMIRAL NAUTILUS.

ANOTHER BRASS HAT SENT OUT FROM ROME!

LOOKS LIKE HE'LL HAVE THE BRASS TO MAKE US FIGHT THOSE GAULS!

LEGIONARIES, I'M HERE TO PUT SOME BACKBONE INTO YOU! DISCIPLINE IS THE STRENGTH OF THE ROMAN ARMY! AND FOR A START...

STAND TO ATTENTION!

YOU DO JUST THAT. BECAUSE WE'RE GOING TO ATTEND TO YOU, ROMANS!

?!

WHOOOSH!

TELL ME, ROMAN, WHY THIS FULL-SCALE ATTACK?

BUT... BUT WE WERE ONLY REHEARSING THE PARADE TO WELCOME ADMIRAL CRUSTACIUS!

THEN TELL YOUR ADMIRAL CRUSTIFERUS THAT IF THERE'S ANY PARADING AROUND HERE...

...WE DO IT!

PAF!

13

NIGHT HAS FALLEN ON THE LITTLE VILLAGE. EVERYONE IS DEEPLY UPSET BY THE INCIDENT. LIGHT SHOWS IN ONLY TWO HUTS...

ONE IS THE HOME OF THE DRUID, WHO IS NOT VERY HOPEFULLY BREWING A POTION OF WHICH HE ALONE KNOWS THE SECRET...

AND THE OTHER IS POOR OBELIX'S HOUSE. HIS FRIEND ASTERIX IS STILL SITTING UP WITH HIM.

IN THE SMALL HOURS...

HAS HE MOVED AT ALL?

I'M AFRAID NOT.

NOW TO WAIT FOR THE POTION TO TAKE EFFECT... AND HOPE!

AREN'T YOU SURE IT WILL WORK, THEN?

I'VE NEVER HAD A CASE LIKE THIS BEFORE... BUT WE MUST LEAVE NO STONE UNTURNED!

WOOF!

YOU'RE THE BEST DRUID IN THE UNIVERSE, GETAFIX! DOGMATIX AND I ARE SURE YOU'LL MANAGE TO CURE OBELIX!

MAY TOUTATIS HEAR YOU, ASTERIX! MAY TOUTATIS HEAR YOU!

15

IN THE ROMAN CAMP OF AQUARIUM...

HERE'S THE ADMIRAL, VICE-ADMIRAL!

ANOTHER OF THE TOP BRASS!

YOU CALL THESE ROMANS? GONE INTO A DECLINE ALREADY, HAVE THEY???

ER... WELL, THE FACT IS...

THE FACT IS WHAT, NAUTILUS?

WELL, YOU SEE, WE WERE JUST PEACEFULLY PARADING...

...WHEN ALL OF A SUDDEN...

ARE YOU SAYING THAT HANDFUL OF GAULS DID THIS TO YOU?

WELL, THEY ARE A HANDFUL... I WAS MUCH STRUCK BY IT MYSELF, ADMIRAL!

NEVER MIND! FOLLOW ME. I HAVE TO TALK TO YOU.

WELL, ADMIRAL CRUSTACIUS, CAN YOU TELL ME WHAT WE'RE DOING IN THIS JUPITER-FORSAKEN COUNTRY?

OUR FLEET IS FOLLOWING CAESAR'S GALLEY AT A DISTANCE. IT IS NOW APPROACHING THE COAST OF ARMORICA, AND OBVIOUSLY THE MUTINEERS WILL TRY TO TAKE REFUGE IN THE VILLAGE OF INDOMITABLE GAULS!

I GET IT! AS SOON AS THEY DISEMBARK AND LEAVE THE SHIP, WE GRAB IT BACK! BRILLIANT IDEA!!!

HO, HO, HO! AND I'LL SOON PERSUADE THE GAULS TO HAND THOSE MUTINEERS OVER!

ER... THAT MIGHT NOT BE SUCH A BRILLIANT IDEA!

STILL NO IMPROVEMENT? NO CHANGE AT ALL!!!

CLICK! LET'S TRY SOMETHING ELSE!

MAYBE A PSYCHOLOGICAL SHOCK... SOME STRONG EMOTION...

I'M SORRY, IMPEDIMENTA... I'D HOPED THAT PERHAPS...

HMPH! AND ME THE BEST COOK IN THE VILLAGE, THOUGH I SAY IT MYSELF!

LET'S TRY ANOTHER EXPERIMENT. PANACEA IS HOME IN THE VILLAGE VISITING HER PARENTS. I'VE ASKED HER TO DROP BY.

PANACEA, MY DEAR, COME IN!

POOR OBELIX! EVEN IN THIS STATE HE RETAINS ALL HIS SEDUCTIVE CHARM!

NO NEED TO OVERDO IT...

SO STONY-HEARTED! I'M HUMILIATED, THOUGH I SAY IT MYSELF!

STILL NO LUCK, ASTERIX.

19

22

THAT ONE OUGHT TO DO!

GNNNNNN!

GNNNNNN!

BOOHOOHOOO! I DID SO WANT TO GIVE PANACEA THIS LOVELY PRESENT!

YOU SEE, DOGMATIX. I'M NOT THE MAN I WAS! I CAN'T EAT THREE MEASLY LITTLE BOARS OR LIFT THE TINIEST LITTLE MENHIR!

WELL, I KNOW WHAT I MUST DO... GO AND LIVE IN THE FOREST ALL BY MYSELF! YOU CAN COME TOO IF YOU LIKE, DOGMATIX!

WOOF!

O GETAFIX, I HAVEN'T SEEN OBELIX FOR HOURS! I'M AFRAID HE MAY BE UP TO SOMETHING SILLY AGAIN!

WELL, AT LEAST HE CAN'T BE DRINKING ANY MORE MAGIC POTION. I'M RIGHT OUT OF STOCK!

BUT WHO KNOWS... THE POTION MIGHT GET HIM BACK TO NORMAL!

I WON'T TAKE THE RISK! OBELIX HAS SUFFERED TOO MANY SEA CHANGES FOR ME TO SEE HIM CHANGE ANY MORE!

MEANWHILE...

THE ADMIRAL'S GETTING ON MY NERVES, INSISTING ON FINDING GAULISH HOSTAGES! I KNOW ONLY TOO WELL WHAT WILL HAPPEN IF WE FIND A SINGLE ONE!

DOGMATIX IS BEHAVING ODDLY! THAT MEANS OBELIX MUST BE IN DANGER!!!

WOOF! WOOF!

YOU WAIT HERE, DOGMATIX. I MUST TELL THE OTHERS!

OBELIX IS IN DANGER!! I'M OFF TO HELP HIM!

THIS MUST BE THE ROMANS' DOING! WE'LL BE WITH YOU, ASTERIX!

WAIT WHILE I MAKE ANOTHER CAULDRON OF POTION! I THINK YOU'RE GOING TO NEED SOME MORE!

SOON AFTERWARDS...

YOU WILL BE AMONG THE FEW VISITORS EVER TO HAVE DRUNK THE MAGIC POTION!

IT'S A GREAT HONOUR FOR US, O VENERABLE DRUID!

AND FINALLY...

DOGMATIX WILL LEAD US STRAIGHT TO OBELIX'S KIDNAPPERS!

SNIFF! SNIFF! SNIFF!

I KNEW IT! THAT'S WHERE OBELIX IS BEING HELD PRISONER!

SURE ENOUGH, THE ADMIRAL'S SHIP, ALL SAILS SET, IS MAKING FOR OSTIA, THE PORT OF ROME, WITH A POOR LITTLE GAUL BELOW DECKS AND FEELING VERY LOW...

SO I GO BACK TO CHILDHOOD! SO I LOSE MY STRENGTH! THE ROMANS AREN'T AFRAID OF ME ANY MORE AND I'M THEIR PRISONER...

OH ASTERIX, PLEASE COME AND HELP ME OUT OF THIS!

WHAT ARE WE WAITING FOR? WE MUST CATCH UP WITH THE ROMAN SHIP AND RESCUE OBELIX!

MY CREW AND I ARE READY TO PURSUE THE ADMIRAL'S GALLEY, ASTERIX!

I'LL COME WITH YOU. I'VE JUST HAD AN IDEA WHICH MIGHT SOLVE POOR OBELIX'S PROBLEMS!

?!

HERE'S YOUR GOURD OF POTION, ASTERIX! I'VE FILLED THIS BARREL TOO, BECAUSE I WON'T BE ABLE TO BREW ANY MORE ON THE VOYAGE!

WE'LL KEEP IT AWAY FROM THE BARRELS OF DRINKING WATER, TO BE ON THE SAFE SIDE!

AND SOON AFTERWARDS...

WE'LL SOON OVERTAKE THE ADMIRAL'S SHIP, THANKS TO THE EFFECTS OF YOUR POTION, O DRUID!

YES, AND ONCE WE'VE RESCUED OBELIX I'LL TELL YOU MY IDEA, ASTERIX!

FLOP! FLOP! FLOP! FLOP! FLOP!

WE SHOULD HAVE CAUGHT UP WITH THE ADMIRAL'S GALLEY AGES AGO, GETAFIX!

YOU'RE RIGHT, IT'S ODD!

WE'VE LEFT THE MARE BRITANNICUM (THE ENGLISH CHANNEL) AND NOW WE'RE ROUNDING THE ISLAND OF SENA (THE ILE DE SEIN), AND WE HAVEN'T SEEN A SAIL ON THE HORIZON! THIS ISN'T NORMAL!

FOR GOOD REASON... THE ADMIRAL'S GALLEY IS ONLY JUST LEAVING THE HARBOUR OF GESOBRNATUM (BREST), WHERE IT WAS HIDDEN FROM SIGHT!

RIGHT, NOW YOU'VE GOT YOUR BOAR!!!

SO EAT UP AND SHUT UP!!!

DON'T WANT BOILED BOAR! WANT ROAST BOAR!

26A

THIS IS TOO MUCH FOR AN ARTIST LIKE ME! I'M THROWING IN MY APRON!

I'LL MURDER HIM! I'LL STRANGLE H.... HRRG! HAAAARF!!! HERRRKK!!!

SAIL AHOY RIGHT AHEAD!

PHEW! AT LAST!

ROMAN SHIP AHOY RIGHT AHEAD!

NO GAULS CELEBRATING THEIR USUAL RITE OF PASSAGE?

26B

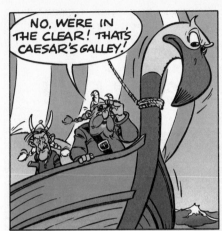

32

33

THE ADMIRAL'S GALLEY CAPTURED BY THE GAULS IS GOING IN THE OPPOSITE DIRECTION FROM THE GALLEY NOW BEING SAILED BY THE PIRATES.

YOU SAID YOU HAD AN IDEA FOR HELPING OBELIX, O DRUID!

THAT'S RIGHT! IT'S TIME TO TAKE AN IMPORTANT DECISION, ASTERIX!

SPARTAKIS, I BELIEVE YOU'RE A GOOD SAILOR?

SO DO I! I'M GREEK, YOU KNOW!

WOULD YOU AND YOUR CREW AGREE TO TAKE US TO A DISTANT ISLAND?

WHAT'S THIS DISTANT ISLAND CALLED?

ATLANTIS!

?!

?

I THOUGHT THAT LEGENDARY CONTINENT SANK BENEATH THE WAVES LONG AGO!

IT DID. BUT A GROUP OF OFFSHORE ISLANDS WAS LEFT.* THE LARGEST IS STILL INHABITED BY THE LAST ATLANTEANS!

* SOMETIMES THOUGHT TO BE THE CANARY ISLANDS.

BUT WHAT DOES THIS ATLANTIS PLACE HAVE TO DO WITH OBELIX?

THE ATLANTEANS ARE DESCENDED FROM A VERY ANCIENT CIVILIZATION, FAR MORE ADVANCED THAN OUR OWN. OBELIX COULD BENEFIT FROM THEIR SKILLS!

WE AGREE, DRUID! WE'LL SET COURSE FOR ATLANTIS! ER...THE CREW WOULDN'T MIND BENEFITING FROM YOUR POTION AGAIN.

OF COURSE!

I'LL FETCH SOME FROM THE RESERVE BARREL!

AND THIS LAST BARREL IS FULL OF WATER TOO... BUT THEN... THAT MUST MEAN...

GETAFIX! WE'VE GOT NO MORE MAGIC POTION!

AND THIS TIME YOU CAN'T BLAME ME!

THIS IS TERRIBLE! WE MUST HAVE LEFT THE BARREL OF POTION BEHIND IN THE OTHER GALLEY'S HOLD!!!

AND NOW IT'S OUT OF REACH!!

NEVER MIND, WE'LL MANAGE WITHOUT! THE VOYAGE WILL TAKE LONGER, THAT'S ALL!

AND SO THE LONG VOYAGE SOUTH BEGINS, A VOYAGE OF NO INTEREST BUT FOR THE FACT THAT IT IS LONG AND OF NO INTEREST.

WE'VE ROUNDED THE COAST OF HISPANIA①, THE COAST OF LUSITANIA②, AND NOW WE'RE SAILING DOWN THE COAST OF AFRICA! WE OUGHT TO BE THERE SOON!

① SPAIN
② PORTUGAL

SURE ENOUGH, AT DAWN...

LAND AHOY! LAND AHOY!!!

32 ᴬ

AT LAST YOU SEE BEFORE YOU THE LEGENDARY ISLAND OF ATLANTIS!

FUNNY WAY OF NAVIGATING!

THESE ATLANTEANS ARE CRAZY!

32 ᴬ

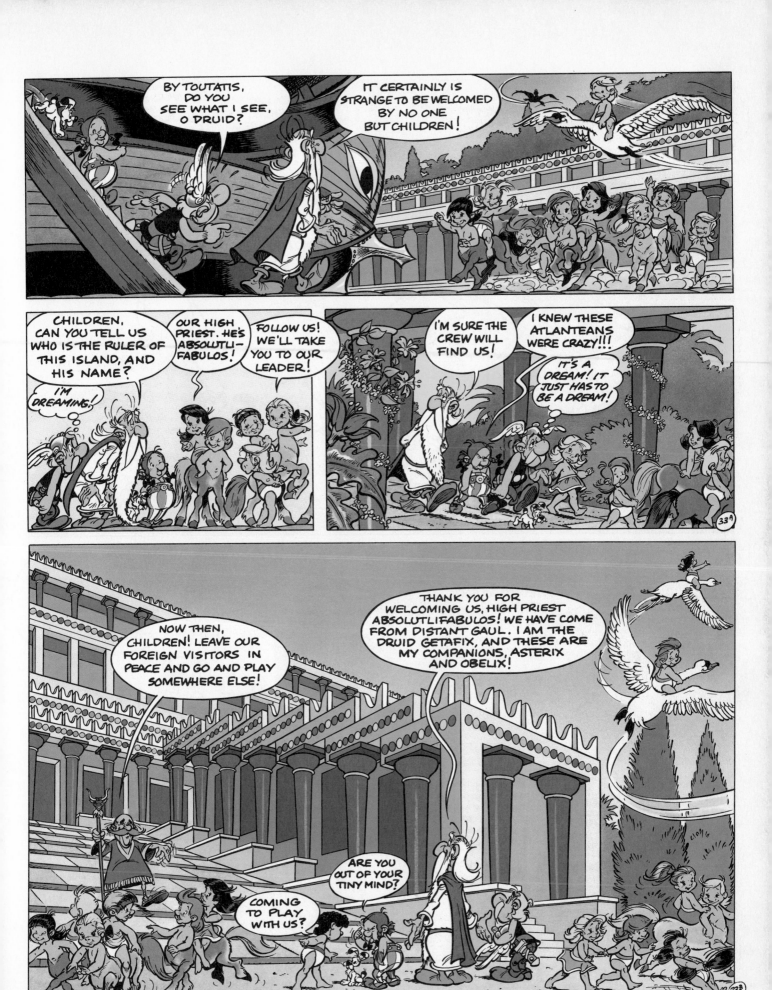

OH DEAR! SO WE CAME ALL THIS WAY FOR NOTHING! WE'LL JUST HAVE TO GO HOME TO OUR VILLAGE!

ALL THE SAME, HIGH PRIEST, I MUST SAY I THINK YOUR SKILLS ARE ABSOLUTELY FABULOUS TOO!

I'M ONLY SORRY THEY'RE NO HELP TO YOU!

SOMETIMES I ENVY OUR FRIEND OBELIX! HE DOESN'T KNOW HOW LUCKY HE IS, GETTING HIS CHILDHOOD BACK! WELL, WE'D BETTER BE OFF. THE CREW WILL BE WAITING.

ER...THE FACT IS...

...IF THE HIGH PRIEST AGREES, THE CREW AND I WOULD LIKE TO STAY. ATLANTIS SEEMS TO BE A LAND OF LIBERTY!

!?

?!

VERY WELL, STRICTLY ON CONDITION THAT OUR GAULISH FRIENDS NEVER REVEAL THE EXISTENCE OF ATLANTIS!

WE SWEAR NEVER TO MENTION IT, ABSOLUTLI-FABULOS!

FLOP!

I'M SURE YOU UNDERSTAND, ASTERIX!

OF COURSE! YOU'LL BE REALLY FREE MEN HERE!

I SAY, OLD BOY, WE HAD SOME GOOD TIMES, WHAT?

IT WAS NICE MEETING A LITTLE BUNDLE OF JOY LIKE YOU... AND YOUR SEA-DOG THERE!

CAN WE ASK YOU ONE MORE FAVOUR, HIGH PRIEST?

I THINK I CAN GUESS WHAT IT IS!

SO NOW WE CAN ONLY RELY ON THE KINDNESS OF AEOLUS* TO GET US HOME.

I FEAR SO.

* GOD OF THE WINDS.

THE INGREDIENTS FOR THE MAGIC POTION AREN'T AVAILABLE ON THIS ISLAND!

WELL, WE STILL HAVE THE CONTENTS OF MY GOURD IF NECESSARY!

IT'S A SHAME YOU'RE GOING! WE HAVE A GREAT TIME HERE!

RRRASP!

41

42

THE SEA HERE IS TEEMING WITH SHARKS... THEY'LL HAVE A FIELD DAY! THROW THIS GAUL WITH THE YELLOW WHISKERS OVERBOARD!

NOOOOO! DON'T DO IT!!! ASTERIX!

ASTERIX!

WITH A ONE...

?

GNNN!

?

AND A TWO...

GNNN!

GNNNNN!

AND A THREE!

I'VE AN IDEA WE'RE GOING TO HAVE FUN AGAIN AT LAST, DOGMATIX!

MUMMMMY!

WOOF WOOF!

AND MY NAME IS OBELIX!

ROW FOR YOUR LIVES!

NO ONE WILL EVER BELIEVE THIS!

44

WHAT THE... HE'S TURNED TO STONE!!!

TAP! TAP! TAP!

THIS MUST BE THE HARDEST WATER EVER!

BUT... BUT NOW I CAN TAKE CAESAR HIS GALLEY BACK ON MY OWN! HE'LL PROMOTE ME TO ADMIRAL AT LEAST!

HOWEVER... AT THIS MOMENT A YOUNG OFFICER AND A CAPTAIN WITHOUT A SHIP ARE ON DUTY IN CHARGE OF THE SECURITY OF OSTIA, THE PORT OF ROME.

LOOK, CAPTAIN! A SHIP FLYING THE PIRATES' ENSIGN IS COMING IN!

LOAD THE BALISTAS!

WHEN I GIVE THE WORD...

FIRE!

SWOOSH!

?!

CRASH!

AVE CAESAR

LET'S BE MAGNANIMOUS AND PICK UP THOSE STUPID, IMPUDENT AND PRETENTIOUS PIRATES!

WHY... WHY, IT'S YOU, VICE ADMIRAL NAUTILUS!

SO IT IS! AND IF YOU WANT TO SEE THE ADMIRAL, HE'S DOWN BELOW!

?

SO STATUES ARE WEARING CLOTHES NOW?

IT'S THE DECADENT LATE ROMAN STYLE!

THIS IS A DISASTER! JULIUS CAESAR'S OWN GALLEY!!!

YES, AND WHICH OF US IS GOING TO TELL HIM ABOUT IT?

NOT VERY FAR FROM HOME NOW, OBELIX!

YOU KNOW, I'D LIKE TO MAKE A LITTLE DETOUR BEFORE WE REACH THE VILLAGE, ASTERIX!

I'VE AN IDEA OBELIX WANTS TO PAY THE CAMP OF AQUARIUM A VISIT.

WELL, WE OWE HIM SOME FUN!

ADMIRAL'S GALLEY IN SIGHT!

HUH! YET ANOTHER BRASS HAT!

WHAT... WHAT ARE THEY DOING?

SNOOZING, YOU BET!

RAISE THE...

IN MEMORY OF THE SILLIEST SAUSAGE IN ROME

HURRY UP! THE LIONS WILL SOON BE BACK ON!

I DON'T UNDERSTAND YOU, CAESAR! YOUR ADMIRAL IS RESPONSIBLE FOR LOSING YOUR GALLEY, AND YOU PUT UP A STATUE TO HIM RIGHT IN THE MIDDLE OF THE ARENA?!

THE LIONS DON'T EAT MUCH GRANITE, IT'S TRUE, BUT NOWADAYS YOU NEVER KNOW. SOMETHING TELLS ME THINGS MIGHT CHANGE, AND THEN MAYBE...

?

TAP! TAP! TAP!

AND A LITTLE LATER AND MUCH FURTHER AWAY, THE VILLAGE OF INDOMITABLE GAULS IS HAPPILY CELEBRATING THE RETURN OF ITS HEROES, ONE OF WHOM IS BACK IN HIS OWN SHAPE... A SHAPE WHICH, AS WE KNOW, IS JUST WELL-COVERED.

DO BE SENSIBLE, OBELIX! YOU'LL HAVE NIGHTMARES AGAIN!

SCRUNCH! NO FEAR OF THAT. SCRUNCH! I HAVE A LOT OF CATCHING UP TO DO.... GULP!

SO IT SEEMS THE MUTINEERS HAVE FOUND ASYLUM IN ANOTHER LAND OF LIBERTY, MY DEAR GETAFIX?

THE ONLY LAND OF LIBERTY I KNOW IS RIGHT UNDER OUR OWN FEET, MY DEAR VITALSTATISTIX!

SCRUNCH! SCRUNCH!

THE END

-UDERZO-96

48

PRINTED IN BELGIUM BY proost INTERNATIONAL BOOK PRODUCTION